Mrs. Muddle's Holidays

Laura F. Nielsen

Pictures by Thomas F. Yezerski

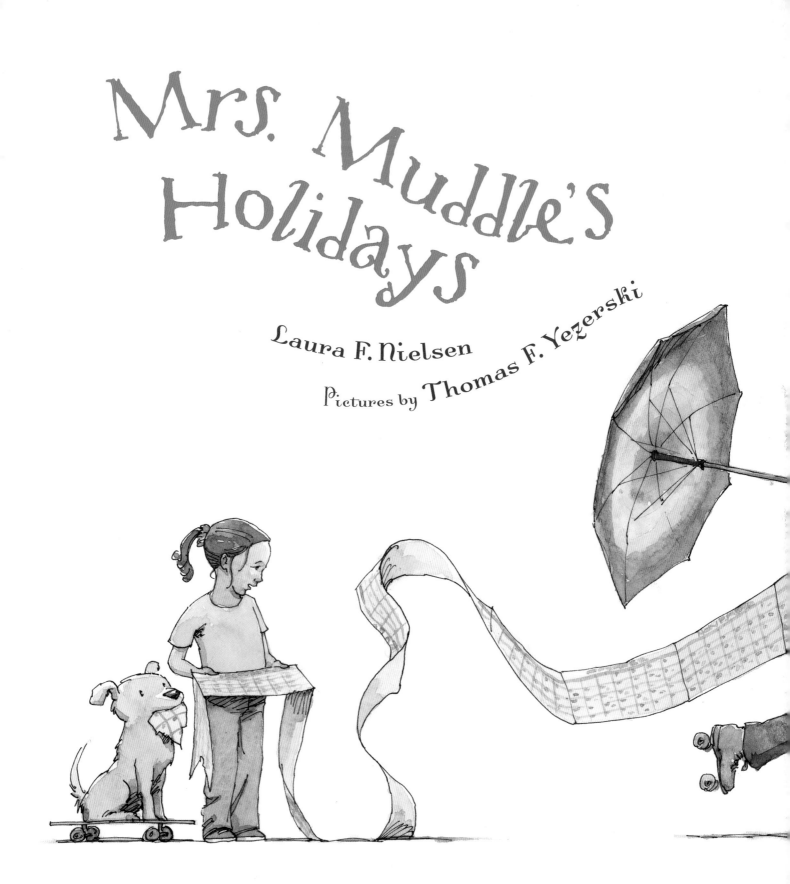

FARRAR STRAUS GIROUX · NEW YORK

To Rosa —L.F.N.
To Mrs. Small —T.F.Y.

Text copyright © 2008 by Laura F. Nielsen
Pictures copyright © 2008 by Thomas F. Yezerski
Distributed in Canada by Douglas & McIntyre Ltd.
Color separations by Embassy Graphics
Printed in Singapore
Designed by Irene Metaxatos
First edition, 2008
1 3 5 7 9 10 8 6 4 2

www.fsgkidsbooks.com

Library of Congress Cataloging-in-Publication Data
Nielsen, Laura F.
    Mrs. Muddle's holidays / Laura F. Nielsen ; pictures by Thomas F. Yezerski.— 1st ed.
        p.   cm.
    Summary: Although accustomed to celebrating nearly all the holidays on the calendar, the Maple
Street neighbors are surprised by the newly-moved-in Mrs. Muddle's definition of a holiday.
    ISBN-13: 978-0-374-35094-9
    ISBN-10: 0-374-35094-9
    [1. Holidays—Fiction.   2. Neighborliness—Fiction.]   I. Yezerski, Thomas, ill.   II. Title.

PZ7.N5674 Mrs 2008
[E]—dc22   2006041287

atie thought that her neighbors on Maple Street celebrated just about every holiday there was. They exchanged valentines in February, hung out flags in July, and carved pumpkins in October.

Many of them celebrated Ramadan,

Rosh Hashanah,

or Christmas.

A few of them even celebrated Patriots' Day,

Arbor Day,

and Pioneer Day.

Then one March, just at the beginning of spring, Mrs. Muddle
moved into the little house at the end of the street.

The very next day, Katie saw Mrs. Muddle out in her front yard hanging bits of colored yarn on the trees and bushes.

"What are you doing?" asked Katie.

"It's First Robin Day," Mrs. Muddle answered.

"What's that?" Katie asked.

"Today I saw the first robin of spring," Mrs. Muddle explained,
"so I'm welcoming the robins back. The yarn is for their nests. Then I'll
make my famous peanut-butter-and-birdseed cookies. Birds love them."
"May I help?" Katie asked.
"Please do," Mrs. Muddle said.

On a soggy day in April, Katie and her neighbor Alicia saw Mrs. Muddle dancing in a puddle holding a beautiful rainbow-colored umbrella.

"What are you doing?" Alicia asked.

"It's the First Shower of April," Mrs. Muddle said. "I *love* April showers! I just finished dancing the Water Waltz. Now I'm going to do the Puddle Plop. Would you like to get your umbrellas and join me?"

"We'd love to," said Katie and Alicia.

On the first Saturday in May, Katie and her friends noticed Mrs. Muddle digging in her garden. "It's Earthworm Appreciation Day," Mrs. Muddle announced. "I'm finding worms to compete in my Earthworm Olympics."

"Can we enter, too?" begged Katie, Alicia, Tony, and Hassan.

"Of course," said Mrs. Muddle. "But you have to find your *own* worms in your *own* gardens."

By noon, all the gardens on Maple Street were dug up, ready for planting. The kids spent the rest of the day determining which worms were the longest, the fattest, the best tunnel-diggers, and the most creative spellers. One of Mrs. Muddle's worms won the Earthworm Derby.

On June 21, Mrs. Muddle was running through her sprinkler in a purple-and-orange polka-dot bathing suit.

"What are you doing?" asked Katie, Alicia, Tony, Hassan, and Rosa.

"It's the First Day of Summer," Mrs. Muddle explained. "I always run through the sprinkler on the First Day of Summer. But it's more fun with friends. Come and join me."

In July, Mrs. Muddle threw her annual Watermelon Bash.

"What do we do?" asked Katie, Alicia, Tony, Hassan, Rosa, Jim, and Jen-Mei.

"See these watermelons? We need to carve faces on them," Mrs. Muddle explained. "This year I want to make them look like my favorite movie stars."

"We can do that," Katie said. "Is there any other way we can help?"

"Of course!" Mrs. Muddle said. "After we carve these faces, we have to eat all this watermelon!"

In August, the kids on Maple Street helped Mrs. Muddle peel, mince, slice, dice, fry, bake, and pickle garlic for her annual Garlic Jubilee.

On September 17, they held a parade to commemorate the Birthday of the Inventor of the Roller Skate.

In October, the kids helped Mrs. Muddle celebrate the First Fire of Fall.

In November, they raked all the leaves in the neighborhood, looking for presents the Leaf Fairy had hidden.

In December, they celebrated
the First Snow.

In January, they held an Ice
Spectacle.

And in February, the whole neighborhood joined Mrs. Muddle in celebrating Let's Pretend It's Summer Day.

"I can't wait for the First Shower of April," Katie told her friends one day. "I just got a beautiful new umbrella."

"I'm designing faces for next year's watermelons," Tony announced. "I want to carve them to look like American presidents."

"I've been practicing on my roller skates," Alicia said. "This year, I *won't* fall down."

"I like Mrs. Muddle's holidays," Katie said, "but I'd like to celebrate a holiday she doesn't know about."

"What holiday is that?" asked Jen-Mei.

"She knows about more holidays than anyone," Hassan added.

"Not this one," Katie said. "Here's my plan. It's going to take a lot of work. We'll need everyone's help."

One morning a few months later, Mrs. Muddle noticed her neighbors behaving oddly. Katie and her mother were tying ribbons around everything, even their dog!

Jim was decorating the mailboxes with balloons.

Alicia and her dad were stringing lights between the lampposts on one side of the street, while Rosa and her brothers strung lights on the other side.

Meanwhile, Hassan was decorating the entire street with sidewalk chalk.

Mrs. Muddle was curious. It looked as if everyone was getting ready for a holiday, but she couldn't imagine which one. She checked her calendar. It was the second Tuesday after the first full moon after the summer solstice . . . but that wasn't a holiday as far as Mrs. Muddle knew.

The parents set up tables and covered them with delicious food.
All the kids gathered around.

Mrs. Muddle couldn't hold back her curiosity any longer.
"What are you doing?" she asked.

"We're celebrating," the children told her.
"I can see that," Mrs. Muddle said. "But what's the big occasion?"

"It's MRS. MUDDLE DAY!" everyone shouted. The lights twinkled. The balloons bobbed in the wind. Katie's dog ran around and barked. The kids got out their kazoos and played a special composition: "The Mrs. Muddle March." Everyone ate and laughed and sang and danced at the biggest celebration Maple Street had ever seen.

Holidays

The word *holiday* comes from the words *holy day*. Many religions observe special holy days. Well-known examples are Christmas and Easter, Rosh Hashanah and Yom Kippur, and the monthlong Ramadan. While some of these observances are prescribed in sacred writings, often other traditions have grown up around these holidays as families and communities celebrate together. The word *holiday* now means any special day of celebration or remembrance.

In the United States, national holidays must be established by an act of Congress. Some of these are Thanksgiving, Mother's Day, and Veterans Day. There are also state holidays. In Massachusetts, the third Monday in April is Patriots' Day, which commemorates Paul Revere's ride and the battles of Lexington and Concord. In Utah, Pioneer Day, July 24, celebrates the arrival of the first pioneers in the Salt Lake Valley. Arbor Day is observed on different dates across the country, depending on when the weather is right for planting trees.

But not every holiday requires an act of Congress. Since the early days of the United States, people have come together at county fairs and rodeos, barn raisings and quilting bees, and town celebrations such as Poultry Day, Trout and Berry Days, or a Lilac Festival. Since the settlers had many different religious and cultural traditions, these events gave them something they could enjoy together. Even today, people are embracing new holidays. Kwanzaa, December 26–January 1, was created in 1966 to honor African American heritage and values, while Earth Day, April 22, was introduced in 1970 to remind people to take care of our planet.

There are more holidays on the calendar than any one person could ever observe. But everyone needs something to celebrate and people to celebrate with. Sometimes the most wonderful occasions are the ones people make for themselves—the birthday party, the family trip, or the neighborhood picnic that becomes bigger and better every year until it becomes a tradition. Mrs. Muddle's holidays are this kind. She is celebrating her favorite things—April showers, the beginning of summer, the first snow. But she is really celebrating friends, community, and love.